I Love You, Nose!

I Love You, Toes!

Linda Davick

BEACH LANE BOOKS • New York London Toronto Sydney New Delhi

Beach Lane Books
An imprint of Simon & Schuster Children's Publishing Division
1230 Avenue of the Americas, New York, New York 10020
Copyright © 2013 by Linda Davick
All rights reserved, including the right of reproduction in whole or in part in any form.
BEACH LANE BOOKS is a trademark of Simon & Schuster, Inc.
For information about special discounts for bulk purchases, please contact Simon &
Schuster Special Sales at 1-866-506-1949 or business@simonandschuster.com.
The Simon & Schuster Speakers Bureau can bring authors to your live event. For more
information or to book an event, contact the Simon & Schuster Speakers Bureau at
1-866-248-3049 or visit our website at www.simonspeakers.com.
Book design by Lauren Rille
The text for this book is set in Filosofia and Gil Sans.
The illustrations for this book are rendered in Photoshop.
Manufactured in China
0113 SCP
First Edition
10 9 8 7 6 5 4 3 2 1
Library of Congress Cataloging-in-Publication Data
Davick, Linda.
I love you, nose! I love you, toes! / Linda Davick.—1st ed.
p. cm.
Summary: In rhyming verse, children celebrate each body part.
ISBN 978-1-4424-6037-9 (hardcover)
ISBN 978-1-4424-6038-6 (eBook)
[1. Stories in rhyme. 2. Human body—Fiction.] I. Title.
PZ8.3.D2658Iam 2013
[E]—dc23
2012006994

I love you, hair
upon my head,
straight or curly,
brown or red.

Long or short
or blond or black,
if you're cut off,
you will come back.

I love you, eyebrows—
eyeballs, too!

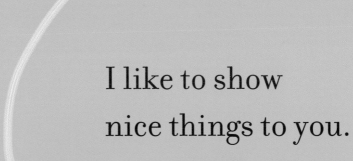

I like to show
nice things to you.

I love you, nose,
though there's no doubt
that when you sneeze
some stuff comes out.

I love you, forehead,
love you, temples.
I love you, cheeks.
I love you, dimples.

I love you, ears.
I love you, chin.
I love you, freckles,
love you, skin.

I love you, neck.
I love you, chest.
I love you, nipples—
east and west.

Wait.

There's a third—
that can't be right.

Oh . . . it's a big
mosquito bite!

hee
hee!

I love you, ribs—
my tickle zone!
I love you, arms
and funny bones.

ha
ha!

I love you, hands.
I love you, hips.
I love you, thumbs
and fingertips.

I love you, tummy.

What's the chance
that we could have
a belly dance?

I love you, back—
you're out of sight!
Can almost hug you,
but not quite.

I love the parts
my friends don't see:
the parts that poop,
the parts that pee.

I love you, legs.
I love you, knees.
You sit down
and stand up for me.

I love you, ankles,
love you, feet.
Toes, you're
good enough to eat!

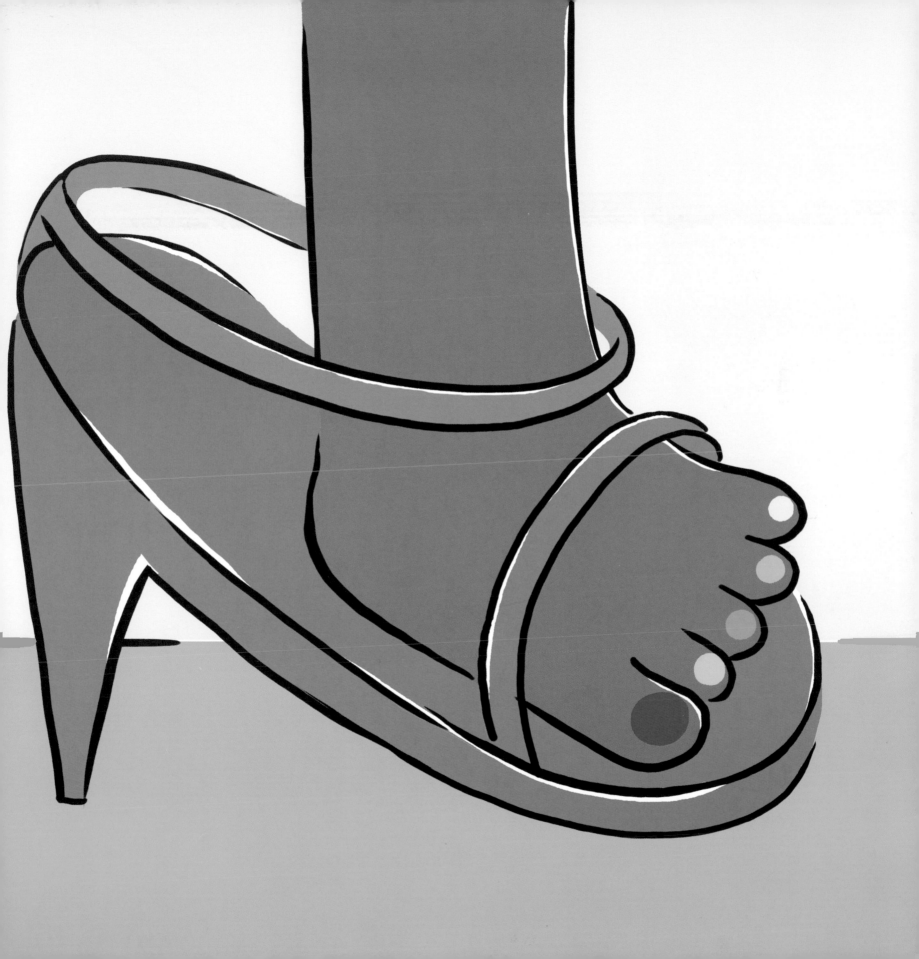

Be careful, body!
Whoa, *beep, beep*!
Make sure to look
before you leap.

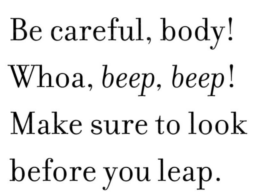

But scratches,
bruises,
come what may,
I'll still love you
anyway.

And at the end
of every day,
there's something that
I like to say:

Good night, eyelids.
Good night, nose.
Good night, fingers.
Good night, toes.

Body, you're
the one for me.
If not for you . . .

w
n . . .

where would I be?